RAISING
LITTLE STRIPE
CARING FOR MONARCHS FROM EGG TO BUTTERFLY

JOYCE HOBERG KAATZ

AUSTIN MACAULEY PUBLISHERS™
LONDON * CAMBRIDGE * NEW YORK * SHARJAH

Ordering Information
Quantity sales: Special discounts are available on quantity purchases by corporations associations, and others. For details, contact the publisher at the address below.

Publisher's Cataloging-in-Publication data
Kaatz, Joyce Hoberg
Raising Little Stripe

ISBN 9781647504205 (Paperback)
ISBN 9781647504212 (Hardback)
ISBN 9781647504229 (ePub e-book)

Library of Congress Control Number: 2020919689

www.austinmacauley.com/us

First Published (2021)
Austin Macauley Publishers LLC
40 Wall Street, 33rd Floor, Suite 3302
New York, NY 10005
USA

mail-usa@austinmacauley.com
+1 (646) 5125767

To my grandchildren: Holden, August, Errol, Mathilda, and Elouise, knowing you will each help save the world by caring for it one step at a time.

I want to thank the many family and friends who have been on this butterfly-raising and story-writing journey with me. Especially: Julie Hample and Candee Kaatz for their creative stories and illustrations and their husbands David and Cory for supporting them during this work; for our grandchildren Holden, August and Errol Hample, Mathilda and Elouise Kaatz, all of whom raised butterflies, spread the word, and believed "of course we can write a book"; for my brother Bill Hoberg who had to put up with a little sister who was not much like him but they did have in common their love of nature; for my parents Pearl and Rolland Hoberg who taught me the love of the land and that I can do anything I set my heart on; and, above all, my husband Brian Kaatz who, for over 45 years, has listened to my ideas, help sort them out to let some ideas disappear and some grow, and never – well, only infrequently – complained about my zoo of caterpillar jars.

So you just found a Monarch egg or caterpillar! Here is a crash course on what to do next:

1. An egg will be milky white or yellow – usually on the underside of a milkweed leaf.

2. Keep the leaf egg side up on a slightly moist paper towel.

3. Check daily for a hatched caterpillar – look for little chew hole on the leaf.

4. Name the caterpillar. Place caterpillar and the leaf in a jar with moist paper towel on bottom. Use netting for cover, and add a stick to give it hope.

5. Clean jar daily, removing leaf, paper towel, and poop – and replace with a clean moist towel. Add a new/fresh milkweed leaf every day.

6. Keep container in a temperature comfortable for you.

7. See where your caterpillar is on the life cycle, at the top of this page.

8. Now you have time to read and enjoy this book and really get to know how to care for your newfound friend, the Monarch.

This book began years ago. My parents allowed me to raise "some" creatures in the house –caterpillars were allowed. As I grew so did my passion for Monarchs. I learned to plant milkweed, start butterfly gardens, and identify eggs. I also saw the challenge of giving impromptu lessons to others about the care of a caterpillar. When my friends and family wanted to care for butterflies, I might attempt to teach them the quick but vital steps. Away they went with a caterpillar only to return with an empty jar to report it did not survive because they forgot an important step. Hence this book. To create Raising Little Stripe, we started to take notes, read the literature, and test our methods. The result is a thorough guide to raising butterflies. And of course, we added a story just for fun.

As you read:

In the yellow box you will learn the vital steps, the "tool box" of
raising your caterpillar from egg to Monarch.

In the blue box is a story. You will enter into the life of Little
Stripe – to follow the butterfly journey through the eyes of a caterpillar.

In Stripe's story look for the butterfly's friend – the lady bug.
And, as always, enjoy!
Joyce Hoberg Kaatz, creator and author
Julie Kaatz Hample, storyline
Candee Fickbohm Kaatz, illustration concepts
Grandchildren, storyline and inspiration

Some people say they don't like it when things change. But for me, I didn't have a choice. My name is Little Stripe. I am a Monarch butterfly. But I wasn't born a butterfly – I changed into one! Let me explain. It began when my great, great, great grandparents started flying north from Mexico to the Midwest. They and their kids flew more than 2,000 miles – what strong butterflies to go so far!

A fun and necessary part of raising Monarchs is providing them with a suitable butterfly habitat (many different flowering plants) including milkweed – a bothersome weed to some people but vital to the Monarch for laying eggs and the only food source for the Monarch caterpillar. Milkweed is not poisonous but it makes Monarchs bad tasting for their enemies to eat.

Now, my grandparents could not land just anywhere when finding a place to live. They had to find milkweed – the only plant where Monarchs lay their eggs. Sadly, milkweed has become harder and harder to find because of, I am told, something called "pesticides" and because the weather and land are changing. Luckily, when it was time for me to be an egg, many families had planted milkweed in their backyard

Plant Milkweed Seeds:
*In the fall by throwing the seeds into the garden or digging them about an inch into the soil. This is the easiest method.
*In the winter by using natural cold stratification. Look that one up!!!
*In the spring by placing the seeds in a container of moist soil, covering them with a plastic bag, refrigerating for three weeks, then putting them under grow lights for six weeks. Plant when the milkweed has two sets of leaves and the soil is free from frost.

Just in the nick of time, my mom found a garden with milkweed for me and flowers with nectar for her. She laid my tiny round cream-colored egg on the underside of a milkweed leaf. I was no bigger than a pin head. Here I was protected from the wind, rain and sun. BUT I was not safe from ants, spiders, wasps, lizards, birds, and other dangers in the garden. These critters were hungry and saw me as one tasty snack.

There are conflicting thoughts about whether human rearing of Monarchs increases their population. Some say just plant more butterfly habitats. Others believe if left alone in nature only 10% of caterpillars survive but if raised by humans, there is a 90% chance of becoming a butterfly. All agree that when "doing it right", raising a few Monarchs for fun and education will create a valuable understanding of this amazing butterfly.

As I started to hatch from my egg and munch on my milkweed leaf, I suddenly heard rustling plants and loud noises coming toward me. I had never heard anything like this before. My world was so new. The leaves around me shook and I saw two huge creatures with arms and claws grabbing for me. The tall creature was called "J.D." and the short creature "Freckles." Could they be the humans I heard about? Oh, my!

"Doing it right" could mean finding a Monarch caterpillar crawling on a leaf in your garden. But it could also mean starting with an unhatched egg. Look for a single egg, creamy yellow in color, size of a pinhead, usually on the bottom side of a milkweed leaf. Break off the leaf and place it in a container on a clean moist towel, egg side up. Change the towel daily to keep it disease free and lightly mist the leaf with water – it will hatch in 3–5 days. Another way to care for an egg, if you have enough milkweed, is to break off the whole top of the plant with the egg on it and place the stem in a container of water. Keep fresh water in the container until the egg hatches.

When these creatures lifted my leaf, I saw a giant pair of big brown eyes and a giant pair of big green eyes looking right at me. Freckles, with the big green eyes, gently tore my leaf off the milkweed stalk, carried me through the garden, over some flowers, up some steps, around a corner, into a porch, and placed my leaf (with me on it!) into a glass jar.

A hatched caterpillar (larva) is very small and may look black. You might find it near little holes on the milkweed leaf where it has begun to eat. Place the leaf with the new baby caterpillar in a CLEAN container that has been washed in a weak bleach solution (about 10% bleach) and rinsed well. The container should be big enough for future wing spread. Adding a wet paper towel to the bottom of the container provides moisture and allows for easy cleanup. Use netting, gauze, or a screen for a lid to provide fresh air.

What a journey that was! At first I felt frightened but once in my jar I felt peaceful and safe. I looked around and saw I had my own stick to climb on, a clean paper towel to lie (and poop) on and plenty of milkweed without all those scary critters seeing me as lunch. I also saw more jars just like mine with smiling caterpillars in them.

Also provide another fresh (no pesticides) milkweed leaf and a stick (in case the caterpillar eventually wants to climb). If you store your container in a place that is a comfortable temperature for you, your caterpillar will also be comfortable. We like to keep our containers outside but protected from sun, rain, and wind. We follow the theory that after August 15 or so caterpillars should be kept outside so they can "fine tune" their radar to get ready to fly south.

As the day went by, I peered out through my jar and watched as J.D. and Freckles put labels on the other jars. The word "Munchie" was written on the jar of a caterpillar who ate all the time, "Sneaky" on a jar where the caterpillar seemed to be hiding, and "Tap Dancer" on a jar where the caterpillar was constantly moving.

You will soon find your project gathers a number of new and old friends who want to help with chores. Let them! (Needed DAILY is a clean and rinsed fresh milkweed leaf, a clean moist paper towel, and a clean poop-free jar). Make sure to wash your hands after handling milkweed since the sap is painful and can cause corneal injury if rubbed into your eyes. There will be discussion and questions (for example: no, it is not black caterpillar eggs on the paper towel, it's poop).

When Freckles approached my jar I anxiously watched to see what name I would be given. There it was written on a piece of tape: "Little Stripe." I was named for my beautiful bright yellow and black stripes – the mark of every Monarch caterpillar. We all felt special and unique with our own names.

Your butterfly "community" will also help you name your caterpillar. Name it as soon as it hatches – she, he, neutral or whatever names – "Tap Dancer, Thor, Bear, Remus, Hot Dog, Gisela, Paulie, Sunny, Little Moon, Compost" – named perhaps after how it acts, where it was found, or in honor of a person or pet who needs a moment of fame.

Every day J.D. and Freckles checked on us. Most days they would carefully lift us from our jars while they cleaned our homes. They would dump out our poop (they called it "frass"), lay down a new moist paper towel, and most importantly give us new clean milkweed to eat. Some days their friends would join them. They would talk about how important we are to nature.

Common community questions: *Can you put several caterpillars in one jar? Yes, but it is harder to know who they are PLUS you need a new milkweed leaf each day for each caterpillar. It is also harder to keep them clean. *What are those other bugs on my milkweed? There are threats around every corner for eggs and caterpillars left in nature. Tiny eggs are eaten by beetles, ants and wasps. Birds also eat them (caterpillar chew marks on leaves give their location away).

We were one big community that kept growing as J.D. and Freckles gathered more eggs and caterpillars. Sometimes they would share one of us with a friend and we would go to a new home. Most days were great. All day long I would eat, poop and sleep with J.D. and Freckles taking care of me and all of my new friends.

*Is it OK to touch a caterpillar? It is safe for humans but ma[y] not for the caterpillar so wash your hands before picking u[p] caterpillar which can be vulnerable to diseases when shed[ding] its skin. *Can you tell if your butterfly will be a boy or a gi[rl]? Yes, the female chrysalis has a tiny vertical line just benea[th] the black dot opposite the gold line. Also the male Monarch [has] 2 black spots on the bottom of its wings and the female d[oes] not. You cannot tell by their jewelry – both boys and girls [wear] "gold chains" on their chrysalis.

I said "most days" because one day was not so great. On that day our enemy the wasp got into the house and we all panicked! J.D. ran around trying to shoo it outside while Freckles made sure all our lids were shut tight. Sneaky hid underneath her leaves even more than usual and Munchie kept nervously eating! Luckily the wasp flew back outside and we could go back to our peaceful life.

After hatching in about 11–18 days your caterpillar may be eating a couple of milkweed leaves a day. It seems like on the two days before it makes a "J", it poops a lot (like it is getting rid of everything it can inside its body before progressing to the next stage of life).

After about two weeks in my jar I was chomping away on my milkweed when I saw the strangest thing! Munchie crawled to the top of his jar and then hung upside down in the shape of a "J". He just hung there all day long. I called out, "What in the world are you doing, Munchie?" But he didn't answer me.

The caterpillar crawls to higher ground (the top of the jar, on a stick, or even on the side of the jar) and spins a silk button to hang from. With its head down it does a twisting dance that helps shed its skin for about the 5th time since becoming a caterpillar. There it stays for about 24 hours before becoming a chrysalis. This is a quiet time for it and you. Clean the container carefully without disturbing it. Just let it be and enjoy the miracle.

Even stranger, the next day I could feel my body telling me it was time for ME to make a "J!" As I crawled up the side of my jar into position, I thought to myself "what in the world are you doing, Little Stripe?" but as I settled into my "J", a peace came over me and I knew it was the right thing to do.

Now more about the miracle: A Monarch can produce 4 generations during one summer. The first 3 generations live 2–6 weeks, mate, go through their life cycle. The 4th generation can live about nine months while flying south. It is easy to remember: a Monarch goes through 4 stages (egg, caterpillar, chrysalis, butterfly), 4 times (generations) a year. It is amazing to realize the first 3 generations only live a few weeks but the final generation lives for months and flies about 2,000 treacherous miles.

After about a day I felt like my body wanted to wiggle and squirm. I wiggled so much my skin fell to the bottom of the jar! My skin was replaced by a beautiful bright green covering. Freckles called me a "chrysalis". My favorite part of my new shell was my shiny gold chain.

A chrysalis can be moved in this stage by: Letting it dry for at least 24 hours, carefully loosen the thread attached to the top of the cage using a tweezer or pin, and attach it to its new home with tape or even a hot–glue gun. Moving it eliminates overcrowding and prevents disease. We can then also watch it more easily. The chrysalis darkens about 48 hours before the butterfly emerges.

As I hung in my new covering, all warm and cozy, I had time to think. I thought of how thankful I was for Freckles, J.D. and their friends who cared for me. And what a miracle that my family could fly so far and change in so many ways. Little did I know what was going on in my body and the changes yet to come for me and my friends.

After about 10 days in the chrysalis, the cuticle (the skin or exoskeleton of the caterpillar) becomes transparent and the Monarch's characteristic orange–and–black wings become visible. The orange color in the wings sends warning to predators that the Monarch is foul tasting and poisonous.

After several days I slowly began to see more than just the darkness of my chrysalis. I could see through the hazy film of my covering. I struggled to use my new body in the sticky stuff around me. I saw the giant, curious, worried eyes of Freckles and his friends watching me struggle. Freckles begged to help me but J.D. said I needed to do it on my own so I could grow stronger for the times ahead.

In the next few hours we witness another wonderful miracle and yet another test of our patience. Just as the struggles we go through as humans often make us stronger, so it is with the butterfly. Struggling to get out of the chrysalis, his heart, lungs and wings become strong. He may look like he is stuck but he can do it. If you help him in any way you could hurt his future and he could die. Don't be tempted to help!

LITTLE STRIPE

Finally I broke free of my chrysalis! I felt the wind through my wings and the sun on my body. I slowly aired myself in the breeze. I saw Freckles' hand gently come next to me and I climbed onto a finger.

What emerges from the chrysalis is a full grown butterfly (there is no such thing as a tiny baby Monarch). Now it is time to say good–bye to your Monarch but you can track her life by tagging her. Local wildlife agencies may tag her or you can purchase a kit with complete instructions. Tagging involves placing a tiny sticker on the Monarch's wing. It can help collect answers to questions about Monarch biology and conservation. It is best to let the butterfly go on a warm sunny day – if you have to keep her inside for a day or two, feed her sugar/honey water.

As I looked around the neighborhood a smile came to my face. I saw many people, just like J.D. and Freckles, who had caught the joy, the passion, of caring for Monarchs. They were planting gardens and fields of flowers and milkweed to save me and my family.

In the past few years, there has been a drastic decline in the Monarch population (down 70–90%). When we care about something or someone it is natural to want to know how we can help them. To start, find out more about how habitat loss, climate change and pesticides/herbicides affect your friend, the Monarch.

As I flew above my new home I saw the faces of Sneaky, Tap Dancer and Munchie now as beautiful butterflies. We all knew our purpose. We would live here in the sweet nectar of the flowers and lay our eggs for the next generation – the generation that would make the long trip south to continue the amazing journey of the Monarch butterfly!

Flying 15–25 miles per hour, your Monarch travels about 2,000 miles to spend winter in California or Mexico depending on what side of the Rockies you are on. They can use warm air and the jet stream to glide. Tagged Monarchs have been found to fly 250 miles a day. A glider pilot saw them 11,000 ft (2 miles) up in the sky. Most birds fly lower than 500 feet when they migrate. We invite you to catch the passion and care for a little piece of the world, starting with caring for the Monarch butterfly.

Joyce Hoberg Kaatz has authored educational and devotional articles; this is her firs
book. Born in Ortonville, Minnesota, her career has been nursing but her passion
is nature. She presently lives between her home on the prairie in Sioux Falls, South
Dakota, and her land on the lake near Park Rapids, Minnesota. Between these
two places, she and her husband have been blessed to raise their children and host
friends and family, foster children, exchange students, and yes, of course, butterflies

CPSIA information can be obtained
at www.ICGtesting.com
Printed in the USA
BVHW020939220221
600768BV00013B/144

9 781647 504212